THE LITTLE
OLD WOMAN
WHO USED HER HEAD

She used her head and she used her head.

The Little Old Woman Who Used Her Head

By
HOPE NEWELL

Pictures by
MARGARET RUSE

New York
THOMAS NELSON AND SONS

PRINTED IN THE UNITED STATES OF AMERICA

TO MY SON

JIMMIE

Contents

THE LITTLE
OLD WOMAN
WHO USED HER HEAD

I. The Little Old Woman

ONCE upon a time there was a Little Old Woman. She lived in a little yellow house with a blue door and two blue window boxes. In each of the window boxes there were yellow tulips.

All around her house was a neat blue fence. Inside the fence was the Little Old Woman's soup garden. She called it a soup garden because she raised vegetables in it, to cook in her soup. She raised carrots, potatoes, turnips, garlic, cabbages and onions.

The Little Old Woman was very poor. If she had not been so clever, she probably could not have made both ends meet. But she was a great one for using her head. She always said, "What is the good of having a head if you don't use it?"

So, as you will see, she managed to get along very well.

II. How She Got a Feather Bed

THE Little Old Woman had only one blanket for her bed. It was a nice red flannel blanket, but it was full of holes.

"I must get a new blanket before winter comes," she said. "Or better yet, I might buy me a feather bed. How warm and cozy I would be in a feather bed on cold winter nights!"

But feather beds cost a lot of money, so the Little Old Woman bought a flock of geese instead. As she was driving them home from the market, she said to herself:

"These twelve geese will lay eggs for me all summer. Then when winter comes I will pluck their feathers and make myself a feather bed. What a clever Old Woman I am!"

When the Little Old Woman arrived home, she drove the geese into the yard and closed the gate. Then she ate her supper and went to bed.

The next morning she heard a great noise in the yard. When she opened the door the geese came running to her.

"Honk, honk!" said the big gander, flapping his wings.

"Honk, honk!" said all the other geese, flapping their wings.

Everywhere she went, the twelve geese followed her, saying, "Honk, honk!" and flapping their wings.

"Dear me," said the Little Old Woman, "I do believe they want something to eat. I must buy them some corn."

So she went to the market and bought a bag of corn for the geese.

Every morning when she opened the door, the geese came running to her.

"Honk, honk!" they said, flapping their wings.

Then she remembered to give them some corn.

The geese ate so much corn that pretty soon the Little Old Woman had to buy another bag of corn. After a while, that bag was empty too, and she had to buy another bag of corn.

"These geese eat a lot of corn," she said, "but after all, they are growing bigger and bigger. Their feathers are growing thicker and thicker. They will make me a fine feather bed when winter comes."

By and by the nights began to grow cold. The red flannel blanket was so full of holes that it did not keep the Little Old Woman warm. She shivered all night long.

"Winter will soon be here," she thought. "It is high time I plucked the geese and made my feather bed."

The next morning she went out to pluck the geese.

"How warm and contented they look," said the Little Old Woman. "They will be cold if I pluck their feathers. Maybe if I cut the holes out of the red blanket, it will be warm enough for me."

But when she fetched her scissors and cut the holes out of the red blanket, the holes were still there. In fact, they were bigger than ever.

"What am I to do?" she thought. "If I take their feathers, the geese will be cold. If I do not take their feathers, I will be cold. I suppose I had better use my head."

And here is how the Little Old Woman used her head.

16

First she tied a wet towel around her forehead. Then she sat down with her forefinger against her nose and shut her eyes.

She used her head and used her head and used her head. She used her head so long that it began to ache, but finally she knew what to do.

"The red blanket is no good to me," she said. "I will cut it into twelve pieces and make each of the geese a warm red coat. Then I can pluck their feathers to make me a feather bed."

The Little Old Woman set to work and made each of the geese a little red coat. On each coat she sewed three shiny brass buttons.

"Now I must pluck the geese and make my feather bed," said the Little Old Woman.

She took a basket and went out to pluck the geese. She plucked the big gander and put his feathers in the basket. She plucked the grey goose and put her feathers into the basket. Then she plucked the other geese and put their feathers into the basket.

When all the geese were plucked, the Little Old Woman put a little red coat on each goose and fastened it with the shiny brass buttons.

"How handsome the geese look," she said. "I was very clever to think of making the little red coats to keep them warm."

Then she carried the basket of feathers into the house and sewed them into a strong ticking to make a feather bed.

When the bed was all finished, the Little Old Woman said to herself:

"I shall sleep very warm this winter. How wise I was to buy a flock of geese to make a feather bed. It all comes of using my head."

III. How She Saved Her Corn

The Little Old Woman was bothered with rats. They gnawed holes in the bag of corn that she kept for the geese, and carried away the corn. They got in the cupboard and ate her victuals. They made nests in her bureau drawers. There were eight of them in all.

"These rats will eat me out of house and home if I am not careful," said the Little Old Woman. "I will catch them in a trap and drown them."

So the Little Old Woman went to the market and bought a large trap. She set the trap and baited it with bacon. Pretty soon she caught a rat.

"So far, so good," said the Little Old Woman. "Now I will drown this rat and catch another one."

But when the rat looked at her with his bright black eyes, she did not like to drown him.

"Poor thing, he looks hungry," she thought. "I will give him a bit of corn before I drown him."

After the rat had eaten the corn, he frisked about in the trap. Then he curled himself up and sat looking at the Little Old Woman with his bright black eyes.

"There is no hurry about drowning the rat," she said. "Besides, I shall be very busy with my baking today. I will drown him tomorrow."

The next morning the Little Old Woman said to herself:

"I must drown that rat today so I can set the trap to catch another one."

But when she went up to the trap, the rat sat up on his hind legs and looked at her with his bright black eyes. She did not like to drown him.

"I shall be very busy in my garden today," thought the Little Old Woman. "Perhaps I had better wait until tomorrow to drown the rat."

The next morning the Little Old Woman said to herself:

"Today I must surely drown that rat so I can set the trap to catch the rest of them. There are seven more rats to catch, and they are eating me out of house and home."

But when she went up to the trap, the rat looked at her with his bright black eyes. Then he sat up on his hind legs and sniffed at her fingers.

"I may as well feed him some corn before I drown him," said the Little Old Woman.

When she brought the corn, the rat ate out of her hand.

"This is a very friendly rat," she said to herself. "I cannot bear to drown him. Perhaps if I open the trap and let him loose, he will run away."

"This is a very friendly rat."

The Little Old Woman opened the trap and turned the rat loose. But the rat did not run away. He came close to her and sat up on his hind legs. He sniffed at her fingers and looked at her with his bright black eyes.

"How tame he is," said the Little Old Woman. "I will keep him for a pet. But I will catch the other rats and drown them."

She set the trap again and baited it with bacon. Pretty soon she caught another rat.

"Now I will drown this one and set the trap to catch another," she said.

But when he looked at her with his bright black eyes, she did not like to drown him either. Instead of drowning him, she fed him some corn.

Every morning she gave him corn, and in a few days he was just as tame as the first rat. Meanwhile, the other six rats were getting into the cupboard and eating her victuals. They were making nests in her bureau drawers. And they were gnawing holes in the bag of corn and carrying away the corn.

"Something will have to be done," said the Little Old Woman. "The six rats I have not caught are eating me out of house and home. But whenever I catch a rat, I cannot bear to drown him. It is high time I used my head."

So the Little Old Woman tied a wet towel around her forehead and sat down with her forefinger against her nose and closed her eyes.

23

She used her head and used her head, and it was not very long before she knew what to do.

"I will catch the rest of the rats, one by one," she said. "When they become tame, I will keep them for pets.

"Every day I will feed them corn so they will not eat my victuals. I will also fix them a nice box to sleep in, so they will not make nests in the bureau drawers."

The Little Old Woman caught the rest of the rats one by one. When they became tame she kept them for pets. At night they slept by the fire in the nice box she had fixed for them. Every morning when she gave them corn, the rats sat up on their hind legs and ate out of her hands.

"Rats make very fine pets," said the Little Old Woman. "How clever I was to tame them. I will have to buy a little extra corn now and again. But it is far better to have eight pet rats than to be eaten out of house and home by wild rats."

IV. How She Kept Her Geese Warm

ONE cold winter night, the Little Old Woman was out in the barn putting her geese to bed. She gave them some corn and took off their little red coats. Then she brushed each little coat with a whisk-broom and carefully shook out the wrinkles.

As she was folding the coats in a neat pile, she thought:

"My poor geese must be very cold at night. I have my cozy fire and my feather bed. But they have not even a blanket to keep them warm."

After the geese had eaten their corn, they began to go to roost.

"Honk, honk!" said the big gander, and he hopped up on the roost.

"Honk, honk!" said the grey goose, and she hopped up on the roost.

"Honk, honk!" said all the other geese, and they hopped up on the roost.

Then the Little Old Woman closed the barn door and went into the house. When she went to bed, she lay awake worrying about the geese. After a while she said to herself:

25

"I cannot sleep a wink for thinking how cold the geese must be. I had better bring them in the house where it is warm."

So the Little Old Woman dressed herself and went out to the barn to fetch the geese. She shooed them off the roost and put on their little red coats. She picked up two geese, and tucking one under each arm, she carried them into the house.

Then she went out to the barn and picked up two more geese. She tucked one goose under each arm and carried them into the house.

When the Little Old Woman had brought all the geese into the house, she said to herself:

"Now I must get them ready for bed again."

She took off their little red coats and gave the geese some corn. Then she brushed each little coat with a whisk-broom and carefully shook out all the wrinkles.

As she was folding the coats in a neat pile, she thought:

"It was very clever of me to bring the geese into the house. Now they will be warm, and I shall be able to sleep."

Then the Little Old Woman undressed herself again and went to bed.

After the geese had eaten their corn, they began to roost.

"Honk, honk!" said the gander, and he hopped up on the foot of the Little Old Woman's bed.

"Honk, honk!" said the grey goose, and she hopped up on the foot of the Little Old Woman's bed.

The geese began to roost.

"Honk, honk!" said all the other geese, and they tried to hop up on the foot of the Little Old Woman's bed.

But it was not a very big bed, and there was not enough room for all the geese to roost. They began to fight. They pushed and shoved each other. They hissed and squawked and flapped their wings.

All night long the geese pushed and shoved each other. All night long they hissed and squawked and flapped their wings.

They made so much noise that the Little Old Woman did not sleep a wink.

"This will never do," she said. "When they were in the barn, I did not sleep for thinking how cold they must be. When they are in the house, I cannot sleep because they make so much noise. Perhaps if I use my head, I shall know what to do."

The Little Old Woman tied a wet towel around her forehead. Then she sat down with her forefinger against her nose and shut her eyes.

She used her head and used her head, and after a while she knew what to do.

"I will move the roost into the house," she said. "The geese will have the cozy fire to keep them warm. Then I will move my bed out into the barn. My feather bed will keep me warm, and I will not be worrying about the geese. They will not keep me awake with their noise. I shall sleep very comfortably in the barn."

The Little Old Woman moved the roost into the house, and she moved her bed out into the barn.

When night came again, she brought the geese into the house. After she had fed them some corn, she took off their little red coats. Then they all hopped up on the roost, and the Little Old Woman went out to the barn to sleep.

Her feather bed kept her as warm as toast. She was not worried about the geese, because she knew that they were warm too. So she slept as sound as a top all night long.

V. How She Saved Her Last Match

WHEN the Little Old Woman looked in her match box one morning, she saw that she had only one match left.

"Dear me," she sighed. "Tomorrow is market day and I cannot buy any more matches until then. I will not let my fire go out, for I must save this match to light my lamp tonight."

As she was eating her breakfast, she thought:

"Since I must keep the fire going all day, I may as well use it. I will heat the flat irons and do my weekly ironing."

After the Little Old Woman had washed and dried her breakfast dishes, she made ready to do her ironing. She set the irons on the stove to heat and laid the ironing board across the backs of two chairs. She fetched a soap box to stand on so she could reach the ironing board.

When the flat irons were hot, she brought out her basket of clothes and began to iron. After she had ironed a few pieces, she began to worry about the match.

"Suppose the match got broken," she thought. "I could not light my lamp tonight. I had better wrap it in a piece of cotton."

31

She set down her iron and plucked a piece of cotton out of the red chair cushion. She wrapped the match in the cotton so it would not get broken.

She laid it carefully in the box and went back to her ironing. After she had ironed a few more pieces, she began to worry about the match again.

"Suppose the match got damp," she thought. "I could not light my lamp tonight. I had better put it in a tin can."

The Little Old Woman set down her iron and went to fetch a tin can. She put the match in the tin can and put a cover on it so it would not get damp. She put the can carefully on the mantelpiece and went back to her ironing.

But after she had ironed quite a few pieces, she began to worry about the match again.

"Maybe it is not a good match and will not light when I strike it," she thought. "Then I could not light my lamp tonight."

The more she thought about it, the more worried she was.

"Dear me," she thought, "I know the match will not get broken, for I have wrapped it in cotton. I know it will not get damp, for I have put it in a tin can. But how am I to know whether it will light when I strike it?"

She worried so much about the match that she forgot to mind her ironing. For a long time she did not iron a single piece. She just stood on the soap box wondering if the match would light. Finally she said:

"This is no way to act. If I go on worrying about the match I shall never get my ironing finished. Maybe if I use my head, I shall find out what to do."

33

So the Little Old Woman tied a wet towel around her head and sat down with her finger against her nose and shut her eyes.

She had hardly used her head any time before she knew what to do.

"How silly I am," chuckled the Little Old Woman. "I should have known what to do without even using my head. I will strike the match this minute and then I'll find out if it will light."

She took the match out of the tin can and unwrapped the cotton from it. Then she struck the match against the mantelpiece.

But it did not light.

She struck it again.

But the match did not light.

She struck it a third time, and the match burst into flame.

As she watched it burn, she said, "This match burns very nicely indeed."

When the match had burned out, the Little Old Woman went back to her ironing.

"Now I will not be worrying about the match," she thought. "I shall be able to mind my ironing."

She ironed and ironed, until by and by the basket was empty. Then she put her ironing board away and set her irons on the back of the stove to cool.

"It is getting dark now," she said to herself. "I had better light my lamp."

The Little Old Woman went back to her ironing.

She filled the lamp with oil and trimmed the wick so that it would burn brightly.

"But now I have no match to light it with," exclaimed the Little Old Woman. "Dear me, perhaps I should have used my head a little longer after all."

After she had thought about it a while, she said:

"Oh, well, I can light a piece of paper from the fire in the stove, and light the lamp from that."

When she had lighted the lamp with a piece of paper, she looked at the big pile of ironing she had done.

"It is just as well that I did strike the match to see if it would light," she said. "Otherwise, I would have worried all day, and I would never have finished so much ironing. I am a very clever Old Woman after all!"

VI. How She Planted Her Garden

ALL winter long the Little Old Woman had saved some tulip bulbs from her window boxes and some onion bulbs from her soup garden for her spring planting. She had kept them safe and dry in a big tin box by the fireplace.

THE LITTLE OLD WOMAN WHO USED HER HEAD

One bright sunny morning, she said to herself: "Spring has come, and I must make ready to plant my tulips and onions."

She tied her red checked apron around her waist and laid out her garden tools. Then she opened the big tin box. She emptied the bulbs out on the table and looked at them.

"Let me see," she thought. "The big brown bulbs are one kind, and the little white bulbs are another kind. I must look sharp so I will know which are tulips and which are onions."

So she put on her glasses and looked sharply at the white bulbs. Then she looked sharply at the brown bulbs. But for the life of her, she could not tell which were tulips and which onions.

"Dear me," she sighed, "I should have tied a red string on my finger so I would remember which were which. How am I to know what kind to plant in the window boxes and what kind to plant in the soup garden?"

The Little Old Woman thought and thought. First she decided that the big brown bulbs were tulips, and the little white bulbs were onions. Then the next minute she was just as sure that the little white bulbs were tulips and the big brown bulbs were onions. But to save her, she could not make up her mind.

"This is a fine mess I have got into," she said. "I shall have to use my head to get myself out of it."

So the Little Old Woman tied a wet towel around her forehead. Then she sat down with her forefinger against her nose and shut her eyes.

39

She used her head and she used her head, and at last she knew what to do.

"How silly of me to get so mixed up," she chuckled. "After all, soup garden bulbs are bound to turn into onions. And surely window box bulbs will know enough to grow into tulips. It does not matter which way I plant them."

So she planted the little white bulbs in the window boxes, and then she planted the big brown bulbs in the soup garden where they would have more room.

"I must remember to water my window boxes," said the Little Old Woman.

She had a little red sprinkling can to water the window boxes, so she tied a red string on her finger to remind her to water them.

"But I must remember to water the soup garden as well," she thought.

So she bought a little blue sprinkling can for the soup garden. Then she tied a blue string on her finger to remind her to water it.

Every day the Little Old Woman watered the window boxes with the little red sprinkling can. Then she watered the soup garden with the little blue sprinkling can.

After a while she saw some little green shoots growing in the window boxes.

"I shall soon have some pretty tulips to look at," she said.

40

When she went out to water the soup garden she saw some little green shoots in it too.

"I shall soon have some nice onions for my soup," she said.

Every morning she looked in the window boxes to see if there were any tulip buds. The green shoots grew taller and taller, but she could not find a bud on them.

Then she would go out in the soup garden and pull up a bulb. But although the bulbs grew bigger and bigger, they did not taste like onions at all.

At last the plants in the window boxes were full grown. They were tall and green, but there was not a sign of a tulip bud among them.

"These plants are no good," said the Little Old Woman. "I will pull them up and plant something else."

So she pulled up one of the bulbs. When she looked at the root, she saw that it was a nice fat onion. She pulled up another plant, and there was another onion.

"This is very strange," she said. "I think I will just have a look at the soup garden plants."

When she looked at the soup garden plants, she could hardly believe her eyes. Every one of them had a lovely yellow tulip blooming on it.

"How pretty they look," said the Little Old Woman. "I was very clever to plant them in the soup garden. I am sure they will be a great treat to the geese and to travelers passing by.

"And how smart I was to plant the onion bulbs in the window boxes. They will be very handy when I need an onion for my soup. What a wise Old Woman I am!"

VII. How She Made Her Apron Longer

The Little Old Woman needed a new apron, but she had no money to buy one.

"If I had a nice piece of calico, I could make myself an apron," she thought. "I will look through my scrap-bag and see what I can find."

So she got out her scrap-bag and put on her spectacles. Then she sat down to look for a piece of calico to make herself an apron.

She opened the bag and began to take out the scraps of calico, one by one.

First she pulled out a piece of blue calico. It was no bigger than a handkerchief.

"This blue calico would make a fine pocket for an apron," she thought. "But what good would an apron pocket be without an apron?"

So she laid it aside and pulled out a piece of red calico. It was quite a long piece, but it was no wider than a necktie.

"This red calico would make me a fine pair of apron

strings," said the Little Old Woman. "But what good would a pair of apron strings be without any apron?"

So she laid aside the red calico and pulled out a very long piece of black calico.

"This piece of black calico would make me a fine apron," she thought. "But it is too long. I am sure that it would drag on the ground. And what good would an apron be if it dragged on the ground?"

So she laid aside the black calico and then she pulled out another piece. This time she pulled out a short piece of purple calico.

"I should like a purple calico apron very much," she said to herself. "But it would be too short. It would not cover my skirt. And what good would an apron be if it did not cover my skirt?"

So the Little Old Woman laid aside the purple calico and went on pulling pieces out of her scrap-bag one by one. Some pieces were too long and some were too short. Some pieces were too wide and some were too narrow. But none of them were the right size to make her an apron.

Finally, there was just one piece of calico left. It was a very pretty piece of yellow calico with green polka dots.

"This is a very fine piece of calico indeed," said the Little Old Woman. "It is not too wide and it is not too narrow and it is not too long. To be sure, it is just a trifle short. However, if

I scrimp and save and cut it sparingly, I do believe it will make me a very fine apron."

So the Little Old Woman fetched her scissors. She scrimped and saved and cut the piece of yellow and green polka dot calico sparingly. Then she held it up against her and looked in the mirror.

"It is not too wide," she said, "and it is not too narrow. It is not too long, but it is just a little bit too short. I must figure out a way to make it longer."

After the Little Old Woman had figured and figured, she said to herself:

"I need another piece of yellow and green polka dot calico to make a ruffle. Then I could sew the ruffle on the bottom of the apron to make it longer. But where am I to get another piece of yellow and green calico? I shall have to use my head for that."

So the Little Old Woman tied a wet towel around her forehead. Then she sat down with her forefinger against her nose and shut her eyes.

She used her head and used her head. Pretty soon she knew where to get another piece of yellow and green polka dot calico.

"I will cut a piece off the top of the apron," she said. "Then I will make it into a ruffle and sew it to the bottom of the apron to make it longer. What a wise Old Woman I am!"

So she took her scissors and cut a piece off the top of the

apron and made a ruffle out of it. She sewed the ruffle on the bottom of the apron to make it longer.

When the apron was all finished, the Little Old Woman put it on and looked in the mirror.

"Dear me," she said. "The apron is shorter than ever. I never would have believed that a ruffle could make an apron shorter! That is something worth knowing.

"Oh, well, I always say you can learn something new every day, if you only use your head."

VIII. How She Finished Her Red Muffler

ONE warm summer morning the Little Old Woman looked out of the door of her little yellow house. She said to herself:

"It is too hot to work in my soup garden today. I will sit down by the window and knit myself a red muffler."

So she took her yarn and knitting needles out of the bureau drawer and put on her spectacles. Then she sat down by the window and began to knit herself a red muffler.

Pretty soon the Little Old Woman's geese wanted to go swimming in a pond not far from the house. They went to the gate and flapped their wings.

"Honk, honk!" they said.

The Little Old Woman got up and put her yarn and knitting needles away in the drawer and took off her spectacles. She went out and opened the gate so the geese could go to the pond.

When all the geese were out of the yard, the Little Old Woman closed the gate and came back to the house. She took her yarn and knitting needles out of the bureau drawer and put on her spectacles. Then she sat down by the window and went on knitting her red muffler.

She had hardly knitted a dozen stitches before the geese came back from the pond. They stood outside the gate flapping their wings and shaking the water off their backs.

"Honk, honk!" they said.

The Little Old Woman got up again. She put her yarn and

knitting needles away in the bureau drawer and took off her spectacles. She went out and opened the gate.

When all the geese were back in the yard, the Little Old Woman closed the gate and came back to the house. She took her yarn and knitting needles out of the drawer and put on her spectacles. Then she sat down by the window and went on knitting her red muffler.

She had hardly knitted a dozen stitches before the geese wanted to go swimming in the pond again. But the Little Old Woman had no sooner let them out of the gate before they wanted to come back in again.

"Dear me," said the Little Old Woman, "I am spending all my time letting the geese in and out of the gate. At this rate, I shall never get my red muffler done. I think I will use my head and find out what to do."

So she tied a wet towel around her head and sat down with her forefinger against her nose and shut her eyes.

She used her head and used her head, and after a while she found out what to do.

"I will saw two holes at the bottom of the gate," said the Little Old Woman. "When the geese want to go to the pond, they can crawl out through one hole. When they come back from the pond after their swim, they can crawl in through the other hole."

So the Little Old Woman fetched her saw and sawed two

49

holes at the bottom of the gate. As she was coming back to the house, she thought:

"Now I will not have to go out to open the gate for the geese. And I shall have my red muffler knitted in no time. What a clever Old Woman I am!"

She took her yarn and knitting needles out of the bureau drawer and put on her spectacles. Then she sat down by the window and went on with her knitting.

Pretty soon the geese wanted to go swimming in the pond. They went to the gate and flapped their wings.

"Honk, honk!" they said.

But the Little Old Woman did not get up. She sat by the window, knitting her red muffler.

The geese flapped their wings again.

"Honk, honk!" they said.

The Little Old Woman paid no attention to them.

After a while, the old gander spied one of the holes in the gate. He crawled through the hole and went to the pond. Soon the grey goose spied the hole in the gate, and she crawled through it and went to the pond. Before long, all the other geese spied the hole in the gate, and they crawled through it and went to the pond.

The Little Old Woman sat by the window knitting her red muffler. She had hardly knitted a dozen stitches before the geese came back from the pond.

"Now they will flap their wings and say, 'Honk, honk!'" said the Little Old Woman. "But I will not get up and open the gate. By and by they will find the other hole and crawl through it."

But the geese did not flap their wings and say, "Honk, honk!" And instead of looking for the other hole, every one of them crawled back in the same way they had crawled out.

"How silly the geese are!" said the Little Old Woman. "Here I have made two holes, and they only use one of them. I might have spared myself all the trouble of making the other hole."

All morning long, the Little Old Woman sat by the window and knitted her red muffler. All morning long, the geese crawled back and forth through the same hole in the gate.

At last the Little Old Woman finished the red muffler. But

the geese were still crawling back and forth through the same hole in the gate.

"It was very clever of me to make two holes after all," said the Little Old Woman. "The geese will have that hole worn out in no time. When it is worn out, the other hole will come in very handy. What a clever Old Woman I am!"

IX. How She Did Her Marketing

ONE day when the Little Old Woman was weeding her soup garden, the pack peddler came along crying his wares.

"Any tacks, laces, nutmeg graters, ribbons, mousetraps or buttons today?" he cried.

The Little Old Woman shook her head.

"No," she said. "I have no money to spare. It is all I can do to make both ends meet."

"Any hairpins, cooking pots, calico, button hooks, needles or spices?" he cried.

But the Little Old Woman shook her head.

"No," she said. "Today is market day, and I must save my money to buy meat and bread for my supper."

"How about a pair of magnifying spectacles?" asked the peddler.

"Magnifying spectacles!" exclaimed the Little Old Woman. "And what may they be?"

"They are a very useful kind of spectacles," the peddler explained. "When you wear them, everything looks twice as large as before."

"How about a pair of magnifying spectacles?"

"But what good are they?" asked the Little Old Woman. "Why should I want things to look twice as big as before?"

"That is easy to answer," the peddler replied. "The larger things are, the more plainly you can see them."

"I never happened to think of that before," said the Little Old Woman. "What you say is very true."

"Why not put the spectacles on, and see for yourself how large things look?" said the peddler.

"Well, I suppose it would do no harm to try them on," she said. "But, mind you, I have no money to buy them."

"Just as you say," said the peddler.

He opened his pack and took out the magnifying spectacles. The Little Old Woman put them on and looked at her soup garden. She could hardly believe her eyes. The cabbages looked twice as big. The tomatoes looked twice as big. Everything in the garden looked twice as big as it had before.

"How my vegetables have grown!" exclaimed the Little Old Woman. "And how plainly I can see them! These are very fine spectacles indeed."

"They are quite cheap, too," said the peddler. "If you should buy them, I am sure they would come in very handy."

"That is just what I was thinking," the Little Old Woman replied. "I will fetch you some money from my china teapot."

She hurried into the house and took some money from out of her china teapot to pay for the spectacles.

After the peddler had gone, she said to herself:

"I should like to look at the soup garden through these spectacles again. But first I must go to market and buy some bread and meat for my supper."

As she was getting ready to go to market, she thought:

"I will take the spectacles with me and wear them while I am doing my marketing. I will be able to see more plainly, and I will get more for my money."

So the Little Old Woman put the magnifying spectacles in her market basket and took them with her. After she reached the market, she put on the spectacles so she could see more plainly. When she went to buy her bread, she said to the baker:

"What fine rolls you have today! They are nearly as large as a loaf of bread. One roll will be all I will need."

She bought one roll and put it in her market basket. Then she went to buy her meat.

"What fine chops you have today," she said to the butcher. "They are nearly as large as a whole roast. One chop will be all I will need."

So she bought one chop and put it in her market basket.

As the Little Old Woman was coming home from market, she said to herself:

"I have never bought so much bread and meat for so little money. These spectacles are very useful indeed."

When she was home again, she set about preparing her supper. She took the roll out of the market basket.

"This roll is too big for one meal," she thought. "I will cut off a piece and save the rest for tomorrow."

After she had cut off a piece of the roll and put the rest away, she took the chop out of her market basket.

59

"This chop is too big also," she thought. "I will cut off a piece and save the rest for tomorrow."

So she cut off a piece of the chop and put the rest of it away.

When she had prepared her supper, the Little Old Woman took off her magnifying spectacles. She put them away carefully, and then sat down to eat.

She looked at the piece of roll. It was no bigger than a thimble. She looked at the piece of chop. It was no bigger than a thimble either.

"Mercy!" cried the Little Old Woman. "What has happened to my supper? There is not enough left to feed a mouse!"

She began to look for the rest of her supper. She looked at her plate. She looked under her plate. But she did not find it. She looked on the table. She looked under the table. But she did not find the rest of her supper.

After she had looked everywhere, she said:

"This is very strange. Something seems to be wrong, and I must use my head to find out what it is."

So she tied a wet towel around her forehead and sat down with her forefinger against her nose and shut her eyes.

She used her head and used her head. Pretty soon she found out what to do.

"What a silly Old Woman I am!" she said. "How can I find my supper when I cannot see plainly? I must put on my magnifying spectacles."

The Little Old Woman got her magnifying spectacles and put them on. Then she came back to the table. She looked at her plate, and there she saw her supper as plainly as anything.

As she sat down to eat, she said to herself:

"It was very wise of me to put on my magnifying spectacles. Now I see my supper very plainly. And what a fine big supper it is, to be sure! I am afraid I shall not be able to eat half of it."

X. How She Rested Her Head

ALL the year round the Little Old Woman used her head to find out what to do.

One evening she said to herself, "How time does fly! It seems only yesterday that I made my geese their little red coats and plucked their feathers to make my feather bed. Now it is fall again.

"I have used my head so much this year that I think I will give it a rest."

So the Little Old Woman sat down in her rocking-chair to rest her head.

"The nights are growing colder," she thought. "I had better sit closer to the fireplace."

She got up and moved her chair closer to the fireplace and sat down again. She folded her arms across her apron and put her feet on her little footstool.

"A fireplace is nice and warm," she said to herself. "I must gather some wood tomorrow so I can make a fire. My fireplace will be even warmer when I build a fire in it. And besides, a fire is so cozy to look at.

"The evenings will be very long now. I shall have plenty of time to sit by my fire and think. I shall think about pleasant things for that will rest my head.

"I shall think how warm my geese are in their little red jackets. I shall think how comfortable my rats are in their little box.

"I shall think how comfortable I am in my feather bed.

"It will be very pleasant to sit by my fire and think how contented and happy we are, and all because I used my head."